I am an ARO PUBLISHING
TEN WORD BOOK.

My ten words are:

goodbye   look
mother   flowers
to   pretty
grandma   take
please   some

FLOWERS

10 WORDS

Story by MIKE and KRIS COX
Pictures by BOB REESE

Goodbye,
mother.

To grandma's,
please.

Look!

Flowers!

Grandma!

Pretty flowers.

Take some flowers.

Goodbye, grandma.

Pretty flowers.

Pretty flowers.

Pretty flowers.